The Clock Tower Ghost

The Clock Tower Ghost

GENE KEMP

illustrated by Carolyn Dinan

FABER AND FABER
London and Boston

First published in 1981
by Faber and Faber Limited
3 Queen Square London WC1N 3AU
Printed in Great Britain by
Redwood Burn Limited
Trowbridge, Wiltshire

Text © Gene Kemp, 1981
Illustrations © Faber and Faber Limited, 1981

British Library Cataloguing in Publication Data

Kemp, Gene
The clock tower ghost.
I. Title
823'.914[J]   PZ7
ISBN 0–571–11767–8

FOR ALLAN, OF COURSE

"... stubborn, unlaid ghost..."

Milton: *Comus*

"From ghoulies and ghosties,
Long-leggity beasties,
Things that go bump in the night,
– And Mandy Phillips –
Good Lord, deliver us."

Gang Song: Addlesbury Primary School

❧ *Contents* ❧

❧ *The Beginning* ❧

A hundred years ago there lived in the middle of England a very rich man. He owned mile upon mile of cornfields, rivers, hills, valleys and woods; small villages full of black and white cottages, and dark towns full of smoking chimneys; sooty factories and little grimy terraced houses built back to back.

He was a proud man and this pride grew greater as he grew richer. He married a beautiful wife, and they had a child, and he loved them, though not nearly as much as he loved himself. He had everything he wanted, except that if he woke up at three o'clock in the morning, as he did sometimes, he felt a small, discontented itch under his heart, and he didn't know why. But he did know that he wanted everybody to see how rich he was. He wanted them to bow down when he walked by and say, "There goes King Cole, the rich man." His name was Mr. Cole, but he liked to be called King Cole.

The discontented itch grew more troublesome, and bothered him sometimes in the afternoon, when he'd had too much to eat at lunch, so he started to think more and more about what he could do to show people how wonderful he was, especially the Earl of Mercia and Lord Middlemore, whose lands marched alongside his.

One day as he rode through his beautiful estate, he came to the top of a high, wooded hill, with a grassy mound on top where nine stones stood in a circle, surrounded by a deep rampart. There he stood for a long time, gazing at the fields and hills all about him. All this land was his, and gained by his own efforts, too, for his father and grandfather had not even owned the tiny cottage he grew up in. But now he was rich, and he owned all this land, all the land as far as the eye could see.

Far away, on a distant hill, a church bell rang out.

A brilliant smile spread over King Cole's face. An idea had come to him. He knew what he was going to do.

On the top of the hill where he was standing, he would build a clock tower – the tallest clock tower in the world – and it should have a carillon of bells to play a tune, his tune.

He sang aloud to the clouds and the trees and the astonished birds, and the song echoed over the valley and to the hills.

> "Rich King Cole was a merry, old soul,
> And a very fine soul was he.
> He built a clock tower,
> To chime every hour,
> At the top of the tower dwelt he."

"And from here," he cried to his horse, who wasn't in the least interested, since he'd just found a juicy crop of grass, "I shall look on everything I own. This land is mine."

It took a long time. Every stone had to be hauled up that hill, from which trees had been torn up by their roots. There was no rest for anyone, for King Cole drove them on despite complaints that the men were worked too hard for too little pay. One day, an old man with a whiskery face like lichenous granite appeared on the hill.

"You'm upsetting 'em," he said.

"What are you talking about?" snapped King Cole.

"You'm tearing down them trees. You'm flattened they vallums. You'm pulled up the old circle. 'Tidn't right."

"Stop moithering, man. You get on with your business and I'll get on with mine."

"You'll be sorry. Mark my words. You'll be sorry."

But King Cole had stopped listening.

One grey, thundery summer day, when the clouds sat sulking on the hills, King Cole entered his tower, followed by a brass band, very important guests, work people and the villagers. The tower was decorated with pennants and strewn with roses, garlands and balloons everywhere. Behind him came his wife and little son. Through the double doors he walked in triumph, beneath the magnificent coat of arms above, with its unicorn, crown and stars, and a plaque, bearing the inscription:

THIS TOWER WAS BUILT BY CYRIL CLAUDE COLE,
KNOWN AS KING COLE,
IN THE YEAR OF OUR LORD 1880.

Beside this was a carved stone with the three Cs intertwined.

King Cole led the way up into the tower, round and round the spiral staircase, his guests following, full of curiosity. There were five floors altogether, each one rightly furnished and decorated, with treasures collected by King Cole. At the heart of the building was the giant clock with its great brass weights. Onward and upward climbed King Cole and his guests, right to the top, where the clock ticked, tock, tock, tock, like the blows of a hammer. Above the floors was the parapet, circling round beneath the four clock faces that looked north, south, east, west. Here, gargoyles sprang out from the walls, birds flew past the windows high above the trees, and the tower's point spun dizzily against the sullen clouds. King Cole looked out from the parapet.

"All this is mine," he whispered to himself. His guests, crowding the narrow parapet, clapped a little nervously. Then King Cole led them down to the ground floor again, where a scrumptious feast had been prepared.

A while later, he held up his glass.

"To the Tower. To the Tower," he cried.

It was almost three o'clock. Glass in hand, he waited.

A deafening clamour rang out, a terrible, tumultuous, ear-bursting hugeness of a noise.

> "Rich King Cole was a merry, old soul,
> And a very fine soul was he......."

rang out the carillon of bells. Then the hour boomed: one, two, three. Everybody cheered, except Cole's wife who didn't like it at all, and his son who was still miserable because his father wouldn't let him have a little kitten he wanted.

Six months later, the rich and famous Mr. Cole was found dead at the bottom of the tower. It was said that he'd flung himself off the parapet.

His wife, who had never cared for him nor the tower, said she never wanted to lay eyes on it again, packed up and went to London, where she married a fat man, with very little money, whom she loved dearly. The son grew up and went to America, where he sold the tower. The new owner intended to move it stone by stone to California, but he had a lot of other interests and forgot all about it.

Untended and unloved, the tower stood alone on its hill. Weeds grew up all around it. Birds nested among the gargoyles. Pigeons flew in and out of the windows, rooks cawed from the parapet. During the Second World War, enemy bombers navigated their planes by it. The great clock was silenced, and the Home Guard had a look-out post there. The carillon was removed and sold by the uninterested owner.

Just one person cared for it, a small boy named Bill. After the war, the clock was started again, and this boy, Bill, used to go with his Dad on Sunday mornings to wind it up. He loved the tower very much.

After a time the boy's father got another job and moved away. But Bill always remembered the clock tower.

Years passed. The tower grew older, shabbier and more sinister. Daring small boys threw stones at the leaded windows and bats flew in the twilight. Very few people went near it.

In the village they said that it was haunted.

❧ The Middle ❧

1

From the day that she was born, Amanda Phillips was awful. People like that pop up from time to time. She was mean, spiteful, greedy and a bully. She enjoyed taking and breaking other people's things, she liked ruining games and felt-tips and pens and rubbers and anything else that you can think of. At home she always grabbed the last helping of jelly or cake or chocolate biscuit without asking, especially if she thought someone else wanted it. She liked to pretend to stroke the cat and then pull his tail instead. She liked making little children cry, by taking their treasures away from them and holding them out of reach, or by pinching them, or tripping them up, or telling horrible, frightening stories to them. She was a terrible boaster, as well. How she boasted. I can run faster than you, climb higher, swim further. My house is better than your house because my father is richer than your father. My telly is the biggest ever. I came top in spelling. I'm cleverer than you are.

Why did people put up with her? Why didn't someone deal with her, put her in her place, and tell her how awful she was? Well, there were two reasons, the first being that she was well and truly brave. If anyone had to coax a large, ferocious dog, who looked as if he were just longing to fasten his enormous teeth into some small child, out of the playground, it was Mandy Phillips they sent for. If anyone had to get a wasp out of a jam jar, it was Mandy Phillips who did it, if anyone had to go to the Head Teacher and felt nervous, it was Mandy Phillips they took with them. If anyone had to go on an errand after dark it was Mandy Phillips they called for. She didn't seem to know what fear was, so she couldn't be frightened.

The second reason why people put up with her was her temper. Her temper was terrible. Whenever things were not as she wanted, she would scream, shout, hit and kick, bang her head on the wall or floor, bite, spit until she got her own way.

I shan't tell you what she looked like, except that she was *not* pretty, and her granny specs usually sat half-way down her nose. Just imagine the sort of face you dislike most. You can draw it if you like. But I can tell you that when she slitted her eyes and her hair started to stand on end, people ran for cover.

Her family were *not* rich, as she said, but gentle and or-dinary, though they hadn't always been quite as quiet as they were at the beginning of this story. Once Mrs. Phil-lips had been a jolly, laughing girl called Marilyn, and Mr. William Phillips, known as Bill, had been a keen footballer, who liked playing practical jokes. But life with Mandy had tamed them. Living with heels drumming on the floor, head banging on the wall, super shrieking in the supermarket had made them settle for a quiet life.

Chris Phillips was like his Dad, a keen footballer. That, and keeping out of his sister's way, were the two main interests in his life, though he also enjoyed collecting things. He had two ambitions, one to get into the school's first eleven (he was in the second at present), and the other to have a bedroom to himself. He hated sharing with Mandy. If he made a collection, she wrecked it, and her idea of fun was to put a frog in his bed, or leave his football boots out for the dustbin men.

But somebody loved Amanda. Peter Norman Phillips, known as Baby Fred, aged eight months, liked the terrible tantrums and gurgled happily at the shrieks and howls of rage. He was a round baby with fat cheeks and wispy curls all over his head. He had a curly grin and hardly ever cried. As a result, Baby Fred was the one person that Mandy was possibly fond of, except herself.

Fishy, the cat, hated her. Fishy was short for Fish Fingers, his favourite food, and he was a thin, fast-moving cat. He had to be. The fact that cats are supposed to have nine lives seemed to make Mandy think that he wouldn't mind losing some of them. Fishy had other ideas, though. He intended to hang on to as many as he could, despite Mandy.

Both Mandy and Chris went to the Cheadlehouse Primary School, Chris in the class above Mandy, although she was bigger than he, as she often reminded him. Their classrooms were far apart, thank goodness, thought Chris. In school he pretended she wasn't there. She was, actually, the most famous child in the school, because of her fearful temper, and also because she had once screamed at the Head Teacher in Assembly, when he'd told her off for pushing and talking.

Chris ignored her and concentrated on his football.

This was the life of the Phillipses up till this time.

It was all about to change.

2

Mandy Phillips sat at the kitchen table, elbows plonked on either side of her porridge bowl, eyes blazing slits behind her granny glasses, bottom lip stuck out, hair sending out electric sparks. Mandy Phillips was about to erupt like a volcano into one of the rages that made her famous throughout the school, and caused her to be known as Mandy Flips, short for Mandy Flips Her Lid. Anger was growing inside her till her skin was tight and ready to burst. Chris, her brother, moved further away in case he got the porridge bowl emptied over his head, which had happened before. Fishy hid under his chair.

Mandy glared at her father, who was still holding the letter, the cause of it all, and bellowed like a bull stuck with a spike.

"I'm not leaving here. You listen to me, Dad. I'm not *leaving HERE!*"

She leapt up in the air, sat down again, crash on her chair, then stirred her porridge so violently that most of Nature's best food for cooler weather blobbed on to the table. Then she burst into tears and roared. Her brother wiped his forehead, which had been showered with flying oats. Her mother wiped the table, which had been covered with flying oats. You can see why they had long ago given up using tablecloths. In his high chair Baby

Fred gurgled happily, waving his spoon, pretty noise, nice Mandy, he thought, though he had no words as yet.

"Now, just you listen to me, Amanda," her father addressed her patiently and wearily. Sometimes he thought her tantrums had aged him before his time.

"No, I'm not going to listen, I don't want to listen. I'm going to school. Nobody's going to stop me being the dragon!"

She grabbed her anorak, rushed through the door, fell over in the hall because she couldn't see where she was going, knocked over a small table, broke a vase and ran sobbing into the morning. Nobody took any notice. The neighbours had seen her going to school before and it had never been a pretty sight. Down the road she sped like a cheetah trying to set up a new world record for fast cats.

"What is she talking about?" Mr. Phillips asked Chris.

"She's the dragon in their form play. Everybody keeps laughing about it, but she's pleased. She has to roar a lot."

Chris put on his anorak, then said:

"Are we really going to leave, Dad? You see, I don't want to leave the team."

"I know, lad. Still, you go to school now, and we'll talk about it this evening."

All that day, at school, Mandy was good. When she arrived she washed her streaky face and tidied her hair, which she hadn't combed that morning anyway. She worked hard, put up her hand for questions instead of shouting out as usual, waited patiently in line when she had to, instead of pushing to the front, didn't take anyone else's lunch, threw away some antique chewing gum stuck to the bottom of her desk, gave out exercise books quietly without shouting their owner's names at the top of her voice, tidied the library without being asked, and returned Cindy Wright's pencil case.

"Mandy Phillips is sickening for something," said her teacher, Miss Pibble, to Mr. Bubble, the next-door teacher, as they drank their mid-morning coffee.

"Mm. Fancy that. Now, if she's sickening for something does that mean she's more sickening or less sickening than usual?"

Miss Pibble looked at him coldly. There were times when she thought he was not quite right in the head and this was one of them. The Head Teacher came over and joined them.

"Did you mention Amanda Phillips? I noticed her in Assembly – I always do – and wondered if she were getting measles. Very blotchy. Worse then usual."

"She's one of the worst children I've ever taught," said Miss Pibble gloomily.

Mandy's performance as the dragon in the afternoon rehearsal was brilliant. She acted like someone sentenced to prison afterwards, for ever.

Then she loped home, looking so ferocious that people moved out of her way, and one toddler began to cry. Her mind was made up. She was going to settle all this. She wasn't going to be pushed around. She'd show them. Just let them wait and see. Who did they think she was, she'd like to know? Frowning, she worked her way through her food, champing like a machine, gathering her power and energy together into a ball inside her. At last the table was cleared, the washing up done, and Baby Fred put into his cot for the night.

"Now," said their father. They all pulled their chairs close, the others trying not to hear the grinding of Mandy's teeth.

"I've got the chance of a job, an interesting one, in the

clock tower that I've told you about, where my father used to wind up the clock when I was a little boy. The American who owned it has sold it and the new owner wants to make it into a museum, and your mother and I have got the job of organizing and looking after it. It's in a beautiful part of the country, and there's a school close by. We shall be going in a fortnight's time, so think about it, you two, and make up your minds to enjoy it."

Mandy thought about it. Then she shrieked like a steam train letting off a head of steam, flung herself down on the floor, went rigid, drummed her heels and banged her head up and down, thump, thump, thump.

"I don't think she wants to go," shouted Chris above the din.

His father bowed his head in his hands, but Mrs. Phillips got up, walked to the kitchen, filled the bowl with cold water, walked back to the living room and poured it straight over her daughter, who spluttered and choked, sitting up sharply, gasping for air, pulling off her specs. Her mother felt terrible, for she was a gentle person. But she hardened her heart.

"I should have done that years ago," she said. "Now, Amanda, JUST LISTEN TO ME."

Amanda was so astonished that she did.

"We're leaving. It's a chance we can't afford to miss. And it's all settled, so you'll just have to put up with it. I'm sorry you won't be able to be the dragon, and I'm sorry about you, Chris, having to leave the team, but there'll be other plays and other teams in your new school. Now, help me clean up this mess. Everywhere's soaking."

"No! No! No! No! No!" shrieked Mandy and rushed upstairs, dripping all over the place, and flung herself on Chris's bed so that her own would not get wet. She continued to shriek for some time, but since no one came to

tell her to stop it, she gave up in the end, pulled all Chris's bedclothes on the floor and stamped on them, then threw all his toy cars out of the window. Next, into her parents' room where she scrawled, "Pig, pig, pig," all over the mirror with her mother's lipstick.

Later she was made to clear up, but as she did so she screwed up her face, and muttered, "Poloney sausages, crabs and cabbages to cruel monsters." From the way she slitted her eyes at her family as she did so, it was clear whom she meant. When no one was looking she poured Fishy's saucer of milk down the sink. Then she kissed Baby Fred.

"You're the only decent person in this house," she said.

"Burbly, gurgly goo," cooed Fred. He had enjoyed the shriekings.

Later, Mrs. Phillips said she never knew how they got through the next fortnight. There was so much to arrange, to organize and get ready, and through it all, Amanda was giving the performance of a lifetime. She sulked, she threw things, she sat down in the hall and refused to move for two hours, she threw her porridge over Grandma's photograph, she drew on the wallpaper with a purple felt-tip. She came down to breakfast wearing her father's pyjamas and said she was going to school in them, and she carried the cat (struggling all the way, poor animal) to the RSPCA office, round the corner, and told them her father was extremely cruel to cats, and she thought they ought to have it. They were supicious when her mother went to reclaim it, and very slow to believe her when she said he'd never been cruel to an animal in his life.

During that fortnight Amanda had her pocket money stopped, was smacked, sent to bed early, reasoned with, talked to, argued with, nothing made any difference. Eyes like burning slits, bottom lip stuck out, Mandy flipped her lid at home and at school non stop.

"Children, say goodbye to Amanda," said her teacher at the end of the second Friday afternoon. Outside could be heard the sound of "For He's A Jolly Good Fellow" being sung to her brother by his class and the entire second team.

"Goodbye," carolled Mandy's class, wreathed in smiles. They'd come all the way up the school with her and it had been a long time. "Thank goodness," whispered Cindy Brown. "Good riddance to bad rubbish," murmured Lucy Robinson. "I just hope they're as horrible to her as she's been to us," muttered Dave Baxter.

"Here's your folder, Amanda, your work books, and a bar of chocolate from us all." (Miss Pibble always gave those leaving a bar of chocolate.) "And the best of luck in your new school. Good luck to the school as well," she added, but under her breath.

The children left the classroom, Mandy the last. At the doorway she turned and smiled. Miss Pibble thought how touching, in surprise, but not for long. Work books and folder were rammed into the waste bin.

"If I can't be the dragon, you can have that lot," bellowed Mandy Phillips. For a moment she seemed about to cry. Then:

"But I'll keep the chocolate," she shouted and ran out of the school.

Miss Pibble had to sit for a while in the staffroom before she felt strong enough to set off for home. The past fortnight had been most exhausting.

"What's the matter?" asked Mr. Bubble. "Tired?"

"Oh, yes. One day with Amanda Phillips makes me feel a million years old. Oh, I pity wherever it is that she's going. They're welcome to her."

3

Meanwhile, in the depths of the wooded countryside that stretched for mile after mile from the heart of England to the hills of Wales, nocturnal creatures were going about their business, hunting and carrying on generally. The cough of a fox was heard. Stripy badgers trundled through a woodland clearing. An owl hooted and was hooted back at rather cheekily. Bats flew like autumn leaves from the top windows of the clock tower, tall, pointed and lonely on its hill. A cloud drifted across the moon, drawing dark patterns on the ground.

And starting at the foot of the marble staircase, a thin twirl of mist spiralled up the stairs. Somewhere, far off, a dog howled in melancholy despair. Shut out. Again. The staircase filled with air as cold as Siberia, and a vile and appalling smell came wafting up and up and up. A whirring sounded from the giant clock as bong, bong, bong, bong, bong, bong, bong, bong, bong, bong, bong, bong – twelve o'clock arrived.

MIDNIGHT!

THE WITCHING HOUR!

And King Cole materialized out of the wispy mist, and stood, arms outstretched on the parapet, face twisted with pain and hatred, a terrifying figure, and threw himself down, down, down to the ground below, a hundred and eighty metres below, his fearful scream ringing through the midnight air. Splat.

"Oh, oh, ouch," he groaned wearily picking himself off the ground and rubbing his bottom skeleton bone, draped in a muddy grey shroud that didn't cushion his fall at all. "That makes it five thousand, one hundred and forty three times I've done that and every time it hurts a bit more. And my vertigo gets worse. It wasn't too bad at first but now it's awful. Nobody knows how I suffer. Poor King Cole. You were a good chap. You didn't deserve this fate."

He moaned and groaned some more. Several owls screeched in sympathy. Except for one who had an unpleasant, jeering kind of hoot.

"Don't do that," cried King Cole. "You're all right, up there in your tree nest or whatever it is. But I've got to carry on with this horrible leap till I find out the answer to it all. I don't know why, but it's all very exhausting."

At that moment he began to disappear, something which always took him by surprise. The unsympathetic owl jeered again.

"Tuwhit, tuwhoo, more fool you," re-echoed through the dark and tangled woods.

Years of haunting and flinging himself off the tower had weakened King Cole, but failed to change the nastiness of his nature. He seized a lump of rock to heave it at the bird, with a few horrid curses, but, sadly, his hand dematerialized, the rock fell through it and on to his skeleton toe, still visible.

"Ouch," cried the ghost, leaping about. "What a horrible life. Oh, no, I mean . . . " but he didn't have time to finish what he was going to say. He'd disappeared first.

4

To Mandy, peering up through her granny glasses, it seemed that the tower went up for ever and ever till finally, miles away in the sky, it came to a point. And everywhere, there were gargoyles sticking out, head of wolf, head of lion, head of monkey, head of snake. Clouds flew past the top and so did dozens of black, cawing rooks.

"Caw," she said, just like the rooks.

Chris stood silent, clutching a basket from which could be heard irritable mewing sounds. Fishy was not happy. He had been placed in this uncomfortable basket on an old bit of blanket, once used, long ago, by an ancient, long-since-departed dog, whose smell still lingered on. Chris, too, had his doubts, as he gazed at a gargoyle the very image of Mandy.

But the face of Mr. Phillips was aglow. His childhood dreams were coming true. The clock tower he had loved as a boy stood here before him. He was going to live and work in it and at that moment there probably wasn't a happier man in the whole of Western Europe.

"Isn't it wonderful?" he cried. "Isn't it the most beautiful place on earth?"

Mrs. Phillips wasn't nearly so sure about that, hadn't been from the beginning, but, a sensible woman, she was determined to make the best of it.

"Very interesting it will be. A real education for us all," she remarked, getting Baby Fred out of the back of the car, a job usually done by his father, who was, at that moment, gazing at the tower and daydreaming. Fred gurgled happily and waved his starfish hands at the gargoyles. What were they to a baby that loved Amanda? Besides, one looked exactly like her. He blew a bubble at it. "Prrrrrrrrh," he said.

The furniture van drew up behind them, having had some difficulty in negotiating the lanes.

"You left us behind," said Rupert, the driver. "Still, it didn't matter. You can see this place for miles."

"A real landmark," Mr. Phillips said proudly. And with a hand that trembled with excitement he took a key from his pocket, a key so enormous that it had pulled his pocket out of shape, and went towards the huge, arched double door, big enough to allow the furniture van to go through, if neccessary.

"Now," he said, inserting the key into the lock, and pushing, whereupon the door stuck, screeched, and finally opened into two halves. The Phillipses entered, followed by the removal men.

"Not the usual, Reg, is it?" said Rupert.

The room was huge, with a swirling grey floor.

"That's marble," said Mr. Phillips.

"I thought it was plastic," said Mandy. Mrs. Phillips sighed.

Coloured light filtered in through cobwebby, stained-glass windows, too high for them to see out of; it was like being in church. In the centre of the room a glass cylinder rose from floor to ceiling, containing a gigantic brass weight, one of the clock weights.

"Two of them moving up and down in turn operate the clock," explained Mr. Phillips.

This was all very grand, but the same could not be said of the furniture.

"Oh, dear. This is going to take a bit of work. It's worse than I remember," said Mrs. Phillips, looking at an old table lying on its side, a harp with most of its strings broken, and an exceedingly nasty picture of a dead rabbit hanging up over a bowl of fruit. That one, she turned to the wall.

"I can't bear to look at it," she said. Mandy and Chris went to investigate a statue of a Roman soldier, holding his helmet under one arm.

"He hasn't got a head," complained Mandy. "Fancy holding a helmet for a head that isn't there." Perhaps to make up for this some very old heads of deer hung round the walls, with droopy antlers.

"This one died of old age," said Rupert, inspecting its teeth.

"I like this picture," cried Mandy. An aged dog appeared to be dying in the midst of a ruined town. 'After the Plague,' said the inscription underneath.

"You would," said Chris, but under his breath. Mandy was being very amiable today, considering everything, and he had no wish to stir up trouble.

Mrs. Phillips was explaining to Rupert and Reg where the furniture had to go.

"A flat has been fitted out for us on the second and third floors. There are five floors altogether."

"Won't be easy," said Rupert. Together they all passed through another arched doorway at the far end of the ground floor. In front of them rose a spiral staircase with marble steps and a handrail. Up went the small procession, Mr. Phillips now carrying Fred and Chris the cat basket. Fishy complained from time to time.

This floor was different. Very grand. It was empty except that the walls were lined with leather-bound books, some of them chained. But wide bay windows opened out above the trees, stars shone from a blue painted ceiling and a rich carpet lay on the dark, polished floor.

"Perfect," breathed Mr. Phillips.

"Dead boring," thought Mandy.

Up the marble stairs they all continued to the next floor, already converted for them into a kitchen, bathroom and large living room.

"We'll make a start here," said Rupert, taking off his jacket. Leaving Fred and Fishy with Mrs. Phillips, the others continued their upward climb, where on the next floor there were three bedrooms and a tiny one for Baby Fred.

"You mean . . . you mean I can have one all to myself? For my very own, only?" asked Chris, his voice rising right into the air and jumping off for joy. Mandy glared.

"Don't think I enjoyed sharing with you, Horrible," she snapped. "And I'm having first pick."

"Let's toss for it," suggested their father.

Mandy won, but Chris didn't care anyway. He had a room of his own, that was what mattered.

And on once more, to the highest floor, the one just below the clock itself and the parapet.

"I shall call this the armoury," said Mr. Phillips, for the walls were covered with weapons, arrow heads, spears, long bows, cross bows, muskets, rifles and revolvers. "It's a fine collection."

But it wasn't these that held Mandy's attention, though she liked guns and spears, no, it was the strange shapes that stood everywhere, shrouded in grey dust sheets, looking like monsters in soft clay. Down she went on her knees and peered under one.

"It's a suit of armour," she cried, pushing off the grey sheet. Then she sniffed, and shivered.

"Something's died in here, I think. It smells funny, and I've got goose pimples."

"Brrrhhh. It's awfully cold up here, Dad." Chris shivered as well.

"I think it's time we went down and got a warm drink," said his father.

"No, let's go to the top first. It's feeble to give up before we're there," protested Mandy.

"Come on then."

The last arched doorway opened out into daylight, on to the parapet that ran all round the tower, just above the clock whose four faces looked north, south, east, west. Together they looked over the castellated wall that stood between them and the dizzy drop below. You could see . . .

". . . for miles and miles and miles," cried Chris. Mandy looked at him and wondered if she should pretend to push him over, but changed her mind. I am behaving well today, she thought, pleased. Then all of a sudden, her tum was empty. She was famished. Starving. Ravenous. She must eat. Immediately. She told her father so, at the top of her voice.

"All right. All right. Steady down. We'll go and see what your mother packed ready for us."

Mandy remembered quite clearly what her mother had packed, and so, pushing her way to the front, she crashed and banged at high speed, down the winding staircase, shouting.

"Yippee, Yippee, Yippee, I'm a drunken cowboy, Riding on the Wild Prairie," at the top of her voice.

5

Aroused by approaching footsteps, King Cole stirred in

the suit of armour where he spent his days, as it held him together. Fifteenth-century armour from Italy it was, cumbersome and clanky. He'd bought it, at formidable cost, when the tower was new and he'd been proud of it (and the tower). But now he groaned. He felt he was growing into an old ghost, for there were sharp, rheumaticky twinges in his bones, visible or invisible, these days.

He was muttering to himself.

"I thought ghosts weren't supposed to feel things. What rubbish. *I* feel things. Very keenly, in fact. And where's that Crook got to, I should like to know? He's been missing for days. It's just not good enough. I shall complain about him to the Powers That Be."

When King Cole was detailed off by the Powers That Be to haunt the clock tower, he'd been allocated a companion in his loneliness, a ghostly pet, a kind of familiar such as witches have. He'd hoped, as far as he was able, considering his state at the time, for a large black wolf-hound or something of that nature, a fearsome and impressive beast, but no, what he actually got was a tatty-looking, untrustworthy bird, with half its tail feathers missing, known as Crook the Rook. You can tell from the name that he wasn't up to much. King Cole would have preferred a raven. Ravens have dignity, a certain something. Crook had nothing at all. His feathers were untidy, he was always suffering from insect bites, and since hordes of rooks flew in and around the tower, it was difficult to recognize him, except that he was such a mess. Worst of all, he would disappear without warning, which he was not supposed to do. He'd been missing for several days now.

"Most unsatisfactory," grumbled King Cole. "Visitors and workmen everywhere, banging with hammers and things and altering the tower. Something is going on. I

shan't like it. I've made up my mind not to like it."

It was at this point that he heard the footsteps, followed, a few minutes later, by Mandy's face peering under the dustsheet and into the visor. He was, of course, invisible, but she sensed that something was there.

The sight of Mandy's face, weaselly with curiosity, came as a severe shock. After all, he hadn't seen any children for a long time and he'd forgotten what they could be like. He wasn't sure who or what this creature was. could it be ... could it be a demon from deep beneath the earth come to plague him and make his miserable existence even worse?

But the creature went away, and King Cole had sunk back inside the armour, wondering if he'd imagined it all, when Mandy decided to be a cowboy in search of food. The sound of

"Bags first. I bags first. I BAGS ME! Yippee!" was the loudest noise he'd heard since the last thunderstorm.

He shook inside the armour till it rattled.

"I won't have this going on in MY tower!" (He didn't know he no longer owned it.) "This is dreadful, disgusting, d ... d ... d ... diabolical! I must put a stop to this."

He shot out of the armour and floated invisibly down

the spiral staircase, surrounded by his own personal icy cloud, to take a good look at the cause of the disturbance.

6

The cause of the disturbance was in the new kitchen, a jolly room, already fitted with red and white check curtains, a rocking chair and a rag rug. The latticed windows looked out on to the green hills and trees, the swooping birds and the grinning gargoyles. Mrs. Phillips liked it enormously.

So did the cat, Fishy, once he'd recovered from having his feet buttered – a cat's paws must always be buttered when he moves to a new home, because by the time he's licked them clean he's ready to settle down – and when he'd done just that and drunk a saucer of milk, he found the rag rug just his cup of tea or dish of Pretty Cat. Fishy dug his claws into the raggy tufts and purred.

Baby Fred gurgled happily, for such was his nature, home being everywhere and everwhere being home for him. Chris had been promised a game of football with his father when they'd finished unpacking, so he was happy. Mandy couldn't have cared less what the kitchen was like. To her, it was just the usual kind of place where people, PEOPLE, would expect her, HER, AMANDA PHILLIPS, to do draggy, dead boring things like washing up, which she intended to get out of as often as possible. No, what interested Mandy at that moment was the large bar of chocolate her mother had packed with the sandwiches for lunch, and intended for all of them. She had read that soldiers on combat manoeuvres are issued with chocolate for special rations, and moving into the clock tower might be quite a battle, she thought. Mandy wanted all of this large bar. She didn't want anyone else to have any. Chris could have the fruit, much better for him. So, without waiting for anyone else, she grabbed that bar, and tearing off some of the wrapping, stuffed as much as possible into her mouth, wrapping included. Then, quick as a flash, she licked the rest before Chris could fancy it. Ever.

Chris leapt at her, but Mandy dodged, cramming what remained into her mouth, stuffing her cheeks like a hamster, and screwing up her nose at him, chewing away like a chocolate-eating machine.

And that was when King Cole had a really good view of her.

The demon creature was much, much worse than he'd imagined. So horrified was he that he materialized, very briefly.

And she saw him.

Her mouth, full of chocolate goo, opened wide, and at such a sight King Cole vanished back to the safety of his armour, where he shivered and clanked for some time.

"They've thought up a terrible, new punishment for me. Why? Why? What have I done now? What have I done to deserve this fate? I did my best. I wasn't a bad kind of chap. Why should I be pushed off a parapet and then haunted by creatures that look like demons? And where's that wretched bird got to? Never here when he's needed. I need him. I need looking after."

"Hasn't it gone cold?" shivered Mrs. Phillips, down below. "I hope this place isn't going to be draughty. Very nasty things, draughts. They can give your rheumatism, if nothing worse. Mandy, do close your mouth when you eat. And don't take more than your fair share, ever again. You really must learn better manners."

"Ah thaw aw mand," Mandy mouthed through the

chocolate.

"Don't speak with your mouth full, Amanda. Finish what you are eating first."

"My share. That's what she's eating," cried Chris.

"I'll see that you get your fair share. And, Amanda, we're at a new home so let's make a fresh start, shall we? Try to improve your ways. Dear."

Mrs. Phillips hated having to grumble so much.

Waving her arms to aid digestion, Mandy gulped and swallowed, then said:

"I thaw aw man."

"What?"

"A man. I saw a man. Over there. He had a horrid face. All ghostly."

Her mother sighed. "What are you talking about now? Oh, come along, wash your face and we'll start unpacking, and I can show the removal men where to put things. Come on."

The slit-eyed glare was starting.

"I TELL YOU THERE WAS A MAN."

"Nonsense. You're seeing things."

This was too much. Mandy lay down on the rag rug, and began to drum her heels on the new tiles.

"Get up, Amanda." Her father spoke sharply, brought out of a happy day-dream about the tower as a first class museum, full of fascinating objects from all over the world, with people travelling miles to visit it. He came down to earth with a bump. His dream about the clock tower was beginning to come true, but some things were still the same. He still had Mandy for a daughter.

She got up. Then, screaming wildly, she ran to the door and kicked it, leaving a black mark on the white paint. Her toe hurt but she felt much improved and looked round for something else. Rapidly, Chris moved behind his father, and Fishy ran behind the rocking chair. Up above, King Cole listened.

"What a terrifying noise," he thought.

Only Baby Fred, glurking away and banging a spoon, was completely happy.

7

Funnily enough, it was at their new school, not at the clock tower itself, that they first heard about the ghost.

All the family, except for the cat and Baby Fred, were kept so busy unpacking and settling into their strange new home that they were worn out at the end of the day, and slept like logs, Baby Fred a fat, round little log. And the following day, a Tuesday, their mum thought it would be a good idea for Chris and Mandy to stay at home, explore the tower, and sort out their belongings before starting at their new school.

Mandy was at her best worst. She put the cat under the giant clock when it struck mid-day, causing the poor animal to shoot down and round the spiral staircase at cheetah speed, not domestic-animal rate. She hid Chris's football kit under one of the dust sheets in the armoury, where it wasn't found until Mr. Phillips took them all off to inspect what was there, watched evilly by King Cole as he did so, not that he realized this, only he did wonder why the room had gone so cold.

Mandy played lots of other tricks too, but it was this particular one that caused them to be sent off to school the following day instead of having the whole week off. Below the actual clock itself ran a narrow ledge all round the tower, jutting out with no protective wall, only a rope fastened where the person winding the clock could catch cold. It was Mr. Phillips's job to wind the clock from there, once a week. Mrs. Phillips, though normally quite fearless, announced that it frightened her just to look at it, and she would need to be given a million pounds to walk round it.

However, on that Tuesday afternoon, whom should she see but Mandy, holding not the rope but Baby Fred, and pointing out the view to him. He was waving his starfish hands and blowing raspberries. Mandy had recently taught him how to do this and he'd learnt quickly, as babies do.

"Don't call out," whispered Mr. Phillips, coming up beside his wife, who hid her face until it was all over. Safely, she hoped.

There was also another watcher, an angry one, wrapped in his personal, icy cloud.

This dreadful demon creature popped up everywhere. Perhaps it and the mini-demon it carried would fall off? But much to his disappointment they came round quite safely, Mandy being very surefooted and not suffering at all from vertigo. Once down, she was well and truly told off, and the door leading to the ledge safely padlocked except for clock-winding occasions.

"That settles it," said Mrs. Phillips firmly, after she'd hugged Baby Fred very tightly indeed, for of his many admirers she came top of the list. "You're off to school, tomorrow."

Mandy protested but Chris was pleased. He'd explored the clock tower, and now he wanted to find out all about his new school, make friends and play football. Mandy sulked for a while, then set off to find Fishy for a spot of cat-tormenting. But Fishy was far away, watching a rabbit hole. He hadn't encountered wild rabbits before. Had he been a country cat he'd have known that the hole had been deserted for some time. Fishy had a lot to learn as yet. But he was progressing.

The following day Chris and Amanda set off with their father for their new school. He drove them there as it was their first day, but they would have to walk or cycle in future, he said. He took them in and registered them with their new Head Teacher, who was also to be their class teacher.

"What a rotten dump," said Mandy LOUDLY. "I don't think much of this potty little 'ole."

She said this as they entered their new classroom. Twenty-one hate-filled faces glared at her, of course. Chris, horrified, moved as far away as possible, trying to look as if she had nothing to do with him whatsoever, that it was just a coincidence that they'd arrived together.

"I think it's a nice school," he murmured hopefully to no one in particular, praying that someone would hear him and realize that he wasn't like Mandy. Deep inside, though, he was worrying about one thing. This school looked tiny, and he was afraid that there might not be enough boys to make up a team. Chris and Mandy were to be in the same classroom, with its high ceiling and big black stove. They were not to be in the same group, however, thank goodness, thought Chris. Mandy did not even bother to think about it. She was much too busy glaring at them all. Until something caught her eye.

Miss Fairhead was an exciting teacher, and recently the class had compiled a history of the neighbourhood, with folders, classroom books, slides, photographs and large murals on the walls. And as Chris and Mandy looked round their new room they saw...

... the clock tower...

... done in cardboard and painted polystyrene...

... with tissue paper trees all around it...

... with furry animals among the trees...

... and feathery birds in the sky...

... and on the parapet...

... looking straight at them...

... they saw a face...

... not a nice face...

... a strangely familar face...!

... Someone or something clad in long grey draperies...

And Mandy became aware that the children were looking at her with amazement as well as dislike, nudge, nudge, wink, wink. Angry and bewildered Mandy slitted her eyes at them and the grins grew wider, she didn't know why. But Chris, looking from the mural to his sister and back again, understood all right.

Mandy and the strange figure on the parapet were the spitting image of each other ... or as alike as a man or ghost of fifty and a girl of nine could be.

8

Chris found himself beside a pretty girl with a round face, gentle dark eyes and soft dark curls, the complete opposite of Mandy. Her name was Cherry and she helped him sort his books, lent him her rubber and gave him a sweet, sh, don't let Miss know you've got it.

"You look nice," she whispered.

Chris didn't know what to say to that.

"Your sister doesn't."

He didn't know what to say to that, either.

"Is she nice?"

"No," he managed, at last.

"Stop talking, everybody," said Miss Fairhead. "Now, if the new children are settled, we'll start our lesson."

"I'm not settled," thought Mandy. "Shan't ever be settled here. Don't like it. Don't like them. What are they staring at me for? They're making fun of me, laughing at me, that's what they're doing, nasty swedes and turnips that they are. Country kids are thickies and I shall tell 'em so."

As playtime came round, so the boys came round Chris. One had a football.

"Coming to play?" he asked.

"Yeh," answered Chris.

"You're good," one of them, Kevin, said after a bit.

"Got a team?" asked Chris.

"Yeh. A good one. We're top of the small schools' league. And we need a new player, since Joe Mercer left last week. Maybe, you . . . Let's ask Mr. Browning."

"Who's he?"

"Takes the middle class, and our games. He coaches us after school."

Chris grinned. He was happy.

"You know what?" said a girl with a long yellow pigtail, coming up to Mandy.

"No, I don't know what. What's what?" she snapped.

"You . . . look . . . like . . . " said the girl slowly, taking her time, taking her time.

"Like what, for Pete's sake?" asked Mandy irritably. She wasn't sure she wanted to know.

Immediately she was surrounded by children, who half-led, half-pushed her to the painting of the tower, where the girl with the plait took her hand, while Mandy tried to slap her but was prevented, and pointed it to the wraith-like figure.

"Like him," she said simply and they all burst out laughing.

"And who's HIM when he's at home?" She tried to speak jauntily, but, of course, she knew already who he was.

"That ghost, of course, the clock tower ghost. Your ghost now. Didn't you know about him?" Cressy Gale, the girl with the pigtail, was enjoying every minute.

"How do you know the ghost looks like that?" asked Mandy. She knew he did, but she wanted to see if they did, too.

"There's an album over there, full of old pictures and photographs, and he's in it. Horrible he is. Go and look." And Cressy pushed Amanda in the direction of a display table, with various objects on it.

But Mandy side-stepped.

"No thanks. You can keep him," she replied.

"Fancy going to live there," joined in another girl, called Carol Moore. "Your Mum and Dad must be off their rockers, my Mum said. Crazy folks, she said."

A thin girl, with a face that loved nightmares, murmured, "Since you look like him, you're probably related. Your Grandad, is he?"

"Of course he isn't," snapped Mandy. Even more boys and girls gathered round her, jostling. She felt trapped. And inside her, rage began to boil. Nobody, but nobody, trapped Mandy Phillips for long. Who did they think she was? And who did they think they were? She wasn't going to be bullied by this crowd from the sticks, no way.

She blew like a steam whistle with every ounce of her colossal power. Cressy Gale and her cronies fell back and, arms waving like windmills, legs leaping and kicking at high speed, Mandy charged right through the throng, and headed for the wide open spaces outside and the one tree in the playground, which she swung up like a monkey, and sat there glowering at the world, till a teacher, Mr. Browning, blew the whistle for the end of play.

"You're not supposed to go up there, but then you're new, aren't you?" he said, quite kindlily.

She nodded. Then, most unusually for Mandy, who never apologized, she said, "I'm sorry. It was necessary," and stumped back to the classroom.

During the rest of that long, long day, the children decided it was their duty to give her all the gruesome details about the clock tower ghost. How he leapt off the parapet, how he made weird noises and weirder smells, about the groans, the moans and the rattling, how a dead tramp had been found there, an expression of horror on his face, and how the tower had been opened to the public once before, but two visitors had fallen to their deaths, and others had whispered of deadly chills and hands that seemed to push them from behind.

It was not at all cheery. It took all Mandy's determination not to feel depressed.

"Your ghost, that is," said Cressy for possibly the hundredth time.

"You'll be gone in a month. Bet you lot won't be able to stick it, even that long," spoke Carol Moore, prophesying like Old Moore's Almanac. "Yeah, quite soon, now, you lot, you Phillipses will either be dead or gone."

With those kind words, she spat out her chewing gum. On to Mandy's foot. Mandy's jaw jutted out like a seaside pier. She picked up the chewing gum and pressed it carefully on the end of Carol's nose. Carol had a long nose.

"Don't you worry about me, turnip face," she said. "I'll settle that ghost and when I've done that, I'll settle you. For good. Just you wait and see."

9

"How was school?" asked their mother, as mothers do.

"Brilliant," replied Chris.

"Revolting," answered Mandy.

"They say we've got a ghost. There's a picture of it at school," went on Chris.

"Now that's silly talk. How did you get on with your lessons?"

"I did two Maths cards and wrote a story," replied Chris.

"I didn't do anything," said Mandy.

"What were the children like?" persevered Mrs. Phillips.

"Super," replied Chris.

"Revolting," answered Mandy.

It was pretty much as their mother had expected. She gave Baby Fred another spoonful of boiled egg. He beamed his toothless smile at her and glugged.

"The ghost looks like Mandy," announced Chris.

His mother looked up, startled, as well she might be.

"Oh, Chris, now that's a very silly thing to say. Of course the ghost, which we haven't got anyway, doesn't look like Mandy. I've never heard of such a thing."

Mandy pushed away her plate and slipped out of the room, while her mother was busy with Fred's eggy face. Half of her wanted to get out of the washing up, the other half was sad and angry. She thought of her old school, and the dragon play, and she wished she was back there instead of having to go to Addlesbury Primary and endure the tormenting of Cressy Gale and her gang. She decided to go to Chris's room and wreck something, which would help to make her feel better. As she made her way there, the anger inside her sent puffs of nastiness into the tower and the air all around her.

In his suit of armour King Cole sensed this disturbance and decided to investigate. Out he came just in time to materialize in front of Mandy on the staircase, she going up with him going down, parchment face, muddy shroud, the lot. The temperature immediately plummeted to below freezing and in the icy air, Amanda and King Cole stood glaring at each other, face to face, or nearly, as he was rather taller, and standing on a higher step.

"Eeeerrrrrhhhhhoooooowwwwwhhhhhhhhhh!!!!"

"It's a ghost! It's THE ghost!"

"It's a creature! It's THE demon creature!"

"Mummy, Daddy. Help! Where are you?"

"Crook, you useless bird! Where are you? Help."

Not that any of this could be heard, for they were both speechless, eyes goggling, mouths open.

Mandy was the first to move. Down the stairs she scuttled as fast as her skinny legs could carry her.

King Cole shot back to his armour as fast as his skinny legs could carry him. There he quivered and clanked for ages.

The air on the stairs warmed up, and when Mandy arrived with her Mum and Dad, there was no trace of anything at all.

"Ghosts, indeed. I don't care for all this silly talk of yours at all," said her mother, and gave her some extra vitamins, causing Mr. Phillips to say:

"Did you have to, Marilyn? She'll have more energy than ever."

It might seem that Mr. and Mrs. Phillips were being rather slow about all this, that they should have realized that something was really UP, but first of all they were very busy with all the practical details of settling in their new home, starting off the Museum, looking after Baby Fred and so on.

Secondly they'd had Mandy for a few years now, and being used to her ways just thought she was up to something, as usual, perhaps like the time she insisted she wasn't Mandy Phillips at all, but Lady Tormentil Braganza, who lived in a huge mansion called Fantastic Towers, with a park, a swimming pool, six horses, five ponies, four Great Danes, three Persian cats, seven cars, five boats and a helicopter (of her own). That had lasted for a very long fortnight and was most exhausting.

Chris half believed in the ghost, but he was a down-to-earth character, who wished to keep out of trouble and concentrate on his football skills, so he kept quiet.

Friday came at last as Fridays do, thank goodness, and Mandy was pleased to be finished with that week. By now, she had quarrelled with almost the entire school, and collected a number of names, including Four Eyes, Bossy Boots, Vesuvius, Rabbit Face, Boasty Ghosty and Big'ead.

"Nobody, but nobody, in this crummy school is gonna call me names," she hissed through clenched teeth, eyes slitted, hair sending off electric sparks, as she shouted, screamed, spat and kicked her way to fame as usual, this time the fame being that of Best Girl Fighter Ever at Addlesbury Primary.

But there was only one Mandy and seven or eight people in Cressy Gale's gang, plus a few more hangers-on, and those who sat on the fence to see who would win. By this particular Friday Mandy was definitely *not* winning. And Mandy did not enjoy losing.

10

And so, on Friday night Mandy sat up in her bed just before midnight. Of course, she was supposed to be asleep, but had closed her eyes and tried out a snore she'd been practising lately when her mother looked in. Two problems were on her mind and her brain was working away at them like a gerbil with its nuts. First, what was all this ghost business about? The clock tower was obviously haunted, no doubt about that, and what was she going to do about it? And how come she was supposed to look like him, something which really cheesed her off, for she'd always taken it for granted that she was beautiful. She, Mandy Phillips, who was going to be a great actress one day, though she never told anyone about her ambition, was obviously bound to be beautiful. True, she didn't always look anything special in the mirror, but then the mirror was not up to much, none of them were, really. But if she did look like that horrible ghost, then she wasn't beautiful, not at all. Huh, she snorted to herself, they're telling lies, all of them, and turned to the other problem, that of school and the Addlesbury Gang.

How could she stop them bullying her and get round to bullying them instead? That would be super. And quite right and proper, too. Amandas destined to be famous and beautiful shouldn't be bullied by a crowd of vegetables, swedes and turnips, huh. She would settle them, put them in their proper place (grovel, grovel flat on the floor, or on their knees, being humble) and then they would see who was the boss. But how? How to cope with a ghost and a gang?

She took up a book on Kung Fu that she'd borrowed, wondering if she could defeat her enemies by throwing them all around the classroom. That would be interesting. She would walk in on Monday morning and just throw them everywhere, then make them say how sorry they were. She wondered if Miss Fairhead would be surprised at seeing bodies flying through the air. This idea made her much happier, so she reached out for the biscuits and jelly squares she'd sneaked up to bed with her. After that, she'd think about going to sleep, for she now felt confident that she'd win her battle with the Addlesbury Gang next week. She fished out from under her pillow her last remaining furry toy, with only one ear and one leg – all the rest she'd thrown off the parapet to see how fast they fell, and she hadn't fetched them back in again as yet, despite what her mother had said.

The toy had no name. Mandy was not at all soppy.

"You," she said to it, and waggled its head. "I don't look like that stupid ghost, do I?"

The head nodded up and down in agreement.

"Good. Now we'll go to sleep," she said, just as an unearthly scream rent the air, there was a strange flash of greenish light, and the air chilled as a shrouded shape shot past her window. King Cole was carrying out his Friday night duty again.

Mandy rushed to the window and shoved out her head just in time to see the apparition rise, groan and rub its back. She looked round to see if anyone else had seen and heard it, but no one stirred, for the other windows were on the other side of the tower.

"Caw," she exclaimed.

"Crook! You've come back, then," cried the ghost, looking up hopefully, only to see the demon creature's face looking down at him. Hurt with the fall, angry and disappointed, he shook his bony fist at her, and Mandy recognized yet one more enemy, as if she hadn't enough. She shrieked at him:

"That's not nice. Not nice at all."

She seized her wellies, standing by the window, and dropped them on his head. He vanished, his head disappearing last of all, and a hand clutching it. Mandy then stumped back to bed, where she fell fast asleep immediately. As did King Cole in his armour.

And the night settled down to peace and quiet, except for nocturnal prowlers and hunters going about their business. Among those was Crook, flying tower-wards at last, worn out, flying with his eyes closed. He bumped into an owl who was perched on a branch, hungrily watching Fishy, who was watching a hole, which was a set quitted some time ago by a badger. The owl thought Fishy was a rabbit and was just about to swoop when Crook collided with him, and the owl fell off the branch. Disturbed by the various bird noises, bad-tempered ones, Fishy decided to go cat visiting instead of hole-watching, and so, at last, met the love of his life. By the time Crook reached the tower he was so exhausted that he fell asleep on Mandy's heap of toys lying at the bottom.

Next day Mandy told her father and mother all about the remarkable midnight experience. They didn't believe her.

"Just a nightmare, dear," her mother said placidly, and gave her some more vitamin pills. And her father continued to talk about the pots he'd brought back with him from his last expedition.

This so annoyed Mandy that she went to the ground floor and knocked off the head of the Roman soldier that her father had stuck back on again.

11

"And where have you been all this time?" asked King Cole.

Dawn was breaking as Crook at last returned to his official position, perched on the helmet of the suit of armour.

"It's not good enough, you know. You're neglecting your duty. Why, talk about being my familiar, you're never here. Your job is to look after me and keep me company, not to go gadding all over Europe visiting your thousands of relatives."

"Aunt Clara got shut in a cage and we had to get her out," answered Crook sulkily.

"That shouldn't have taken you three months!"

"It's dull here. I do like a bit of life even if I am a ghost bird. Nothing ever happens here except you leaping off the tower, and that gets to be extremely boring after the first fifty years. Besides, I'm used to a large family and lots of chat. I miss it all."

"There are hundreds of rooks round here. Place is littered with rooks. Chat to them."

"Never. They're Norman, and my family's Saxon. There was a great Rook Battle in . . . when was it? Ten sixty six or something like that. That's when I got . . . the chop. We Saxon Rooks never talk to Norman Rooks. Nasty crowd. Can't trust them with half a worm."

"All right. Don't go on and on about it. Now you are here, I'll tell you what's been happening."

"Nothing, most probably."

"Nonsense. It's all happening. A demon creature has moved into the clock tower and I want you to help me get rid of it."

"Try smiling at it. That's enough to frighten a ghost away. Ho, ho, get it?"

"This is no laughing matter. I'm in deadly earnest."

"I know you're deadly, but who's Ernest, poor chap? He didn't deserve to be that unlucky."

"That's enough, Crook!"

"Sorry, master."

"Come along, now. We have to work out a plan."

Crook sighed. "I'm listening."

King Cole's plans were simple. He intended to drive away the Phillips family and the demon creature. Unfortunately he had no idea what that demon creature was like.

Next morning, he was there in the kitchen, evil and invisible (he always found it difficult to materialize between six a.m. and noon). They were having their breakfast. Baby Fred saw him clearly, and waved one podgy mitt at him, and banged his rusk with the other. "Glug, glug," he explained to the rest of the family.

King Cole threw the odd cup and saucer through the air. He'd heard this frightened people out of their minds.

"Don't do that, Mandy," said her mother, catching them deftly, and returning to reading a catalogue that had just arrived. 'What the Well-Equipped Museum Must Have in It," ran the title.

The ghost picked up Mandy's porridge bowl and hurled it at the rag rug where Fishy was crashed out after a night spent serenading his new lady love.

"Oh no, not again, Mandy, protested Mrs. Phillips. "I'd have thought you'd grown out of that messy habit by now. And I wish you wouldn't ask for porridge if you don't want to eat it. I don't enjoy making it, you know. Brrh. It's jolly cold in here. Now, just wipe it up while I fetch my cardy."

"I didn't throw it," growled Mandy in a dangerous voice.

Mr. Phillips didn't even look up from the local newspaper he was reading. Actually he was admiring the ad. he'd put in.

ADDLESBURY TOWER.

THE TOWER THAT MAKES YOU WELCOME.

Museum. Antiquities. Refreshments. Climb the spiral staircase. See the panoramic views. Information. Education. Entertainment.

"Not even a mention of me," thought King Cole, reading it over his shoulder. He looked round, trying to find something really frightful to do. Mrs. Phillips hurried in, wearing her thickest cardigan.

"The clock's stopped. You'll be late for school if you don't hurry. Mandy, you needn't wipe up the porridge this time, but try to control your tantrums or you'll get into trouble. Hurry along, now."

Mandy shook her fists in the air. "But I didn't do anything. It was that ghost, I tell you."

That ghost was trying to pick up an old meat dish from the dresser, the kind dating from the good old days when some lucky people ate tons of meat and so it weighed a ton. Crook, not helping at all, perched on the top shelf.

"Don't start all that rubbish about ghosts again, Mandy," said her father.

"I mustn't be late," Chris was shouting. "Mr. Browning is talking to the team before school and I've just got to be there."

He grabbed his kit and shot straight through King Cole as if he were a ball and the ghost goal posts. Surprised, King Cole dropped the meat dish. Straight on to Mr. Phillips's big toe. The left one.

"Ouch. Ouch. Ouch, ouch, ouch," he bellowed, hopping mad of course. "Do you children have to be quite so rough? Be more careful. It's lucky it didn't smash everywhere."

"Are you blind as well as stupid?" shrieked Mandy, for King Cole had materialized in sheer terror and collapsed into the rocking chair, which rocked violently to and fro. This proved too much for him, and before Dad, Mum or Chris had seen him he vanished back to the safety of the armour, followed closely by Crook.

Despite a rotten start, the Phillipses got on with the day's activity, which for Baby Fred was the important job of producing two front teeth (for central eating, of course).

Mandy had a dreadful day. So did those who had to put up with her temper.

"What we need is something really and truly horrific, like those spooky films," announced Crook, and then wished he hadn't because it took ages to explain to King Cole all about the cinema, moving films, television and so on. And it was clear that when he'd finished King Cole did not believe him.

"Just think of it as a magic lantern," said Crook, giving up. "And what we've really got to think out is what we do next. Dish-throwing frightened you more than it did them. Could you jump off the parapet more often?"

"Oh, dear me, no. It scares me stiff."

"Well, it would," said Crook. "No, it's got to be something spectacular to frighten that girl. She's tough."

"What girl?"

"The one you call the demon creature."

"That's not a girl!"

"She is."

"It can't be. It wears trousers."

"They do."

"It can't be a girl. How they must have changed since my day."

"They have."

"And it's so ugly."

"I wouldn't say that. She looks like you, as a matter of fact."

King Cole was rattling like a chain in the wind.

"Never, never, never. I don't believe you. Stop tormenting me. I was a fine-looking man in my youth."

"You've changed, old boy. And so have girls. Anyway, enough of this. We must make some plans."

That demon creature was also making plans. With bad temper transforming into energy, Mandy was plotting in three directions: school, for the gang had been terrible that day; the ghost, she was going to deal with him; her family, to prove to them that he existed. To fortify herself, she decided she would need some nourishment from Mum's latest hiding place. She found it easily. Poor old Mum. She'd no imagination.

An hour later, the October evening already dark and the wind beginning to sigh and whistle round the tower, a vile aroma started to drift down the spiral staircase, a mixture of rotten cabbage, burnt rubber, and silage. The family were all in the kitchen doing various jobs, except for Fred, in bed, and Fishy, out courting. Mandy sniffed the air.

"That's the ghost coming," she cried. "NOW LOOK OUT, ALL OF YOU. You must see him, this time."

All her family sighed heavily and pretended not to notice. She was off again. Enough to send anybody round the bend, thought Chris, settling back to his Rothman's Football Year Book.

"I think the drain needs unblocking," said Dad. "I'll go down and fix it."

"It's the ghost," Mandy seethed with fury. "You can smell him."

"Well, I've caught cold with all these draughts," said her mother, "and I can't smell a thing. I can't taste any-thing, either."

"Oh, you lot will drive me mad," Mandy shouted, storming out of the kitchen, and up to her bedroom, where an idea hit her, wham.

Down the staircase came King Cole, black cloak (found in an old chest) over his muddy shroud, mask on his face (a vampire one, put on crooked) and a rusty chain clank-ing behind him (making him very slow), arms and hands outstretched, moaning Woe, Woe and Doom, Doom alternately, Crook perched on one shoulder cawing at intervals (and feeling a complete twit). They had worked really hard on their new image, and hoped it would do the trick, filling the Phillipses with utter terror so that they rushed out of the clock tower and into the night, never to darken its door again.

That's what they hoped.

Nearly at the bend just before the kitchen, King Cole paused, ready to burst in for the final fright, and at that moment a really terrifying figure leapt down from the stairs crying, "Stick 'em Up!" Mandy, dressed in her witch's costume for the Hallowe'en party at school, and carrying a water pistol was right behind them. King Cole turned in surprise and received a jet of water in his right eye.

Mandy shrieked to her family, "Come on, come on, quick, he's here."

By the time they arrived all that could be seen on the stairs was a length of chain, a black cloak and a water-soaked mask.

"I wish you didn't make such a mess when you play your games," her mother remarked as she picked them up.

"Pchah," snapped Mandy, stomping back upstairs.

12

Entering into the spirit of the thing, King Cole now appeared and disappeared all over the clock tower, accompanied by a miserable and complaining Crook. Crockery flew through the air, furniture and armour slid through rooms, bloodstains dripped on the spiral stairs, then vanished without trace. Mists murked, draughts froze feet, the tower smelt like a badly kept farmyard on a wet day.

Mandy met King Cole all over the place.

But as for the rest of the family, Mr. Phillips was away

for a week, gathering more antiquities for his Museum, and Mrs. Phillips's cold grew worse, making her deaf, and unable to smell anything at all, and furthermore she put down her glasses somewhere, couldn't find them afterwards and, as a result, couldn't see a thing. Chris? Well, Chris walked in a dream. Chris was over the moon. He didn't care what was going on in the tower. Chris had scored a hat trick in the last match. People were saying that Chris Phillips was the best thing that ever happened to Addlesbury Primary football. Up Addlesbury Primary. Addlesbury Rules OK. Up Chris Phillips. Chris Phillips Rules OK. (Mandy Phillips a load of rubbish but who cares, anyway?) So he noticed nothing.

Fishy knew. Cats always know about things like King Cole. As far as he was concerned, that thing was nasty, just like Mandy, and to be avoided, just like Mandy. Very like, really. What did interest him was the feathery friend who had appeared just lately, because it was satisfactory to know that there were reserves of food in the tower if there was a siege or Mistress Phillips grew mean with the Pretty Cat. But really he was far more interested in his new girl-friend, a gorgeous tortoiseshell called Bomber (her owners hadn't yet realized that tortoiseshell cats are always females), than in ghostly goings-on in the tower. So it was up to Mandy.

And she had not been idle. All the week she had been collecting nettles, brambles and gorse, making a prickly heap at the bottom of the tower ready for the Friday leap. She'd wrecked her mother's best leather gloves doing so, but didn't think her mother would mind.

On Friday night she prepared to stay awake with a book on judo, two bars of chocolate, a bag of boiled sweets, and a selection of fruit that was meant to last for the whole weekend. As the witching hour drew near she seated herself beside the window ready for the action.

As an actor herself, she had to admit he did well. His expression and the things he said as he rose from the heap were brilliant, she thought, and gave him a little clap – not too loud in case the others heard – before she up-ended a bag of flour over him. She felt he'd had enough water with the pistol she'd been using.

Drearily the ghost and Crook returned to the armour, which Mandy had generously covered with itching powder. Before she finally went to sleep, she crept up and played him one of her favourite rock records on her cassette player.

King Cole, aged a hundred and fifty, hadn't known about itching powder or cassette tapes. But he was learning.

13

Mr. Phillips returned with some stuffed animals and what looked like a lot of old pots of poor shape and worse colour. But he was pleased with them. Mandy found the animals far more exciting. She told him all about her week and her battle with the ghost.

"You're got a marvellous imagination, Mandy. You ought to write it all down. Become an author."

Mandy growled and stomped off in disgust, searching for something wicked to do. How could grown-ups be so unbelievably stupid? Who wants to write about a battle when you've got to fight one? As she rummaged in the kitchen for something to smash she found her Mum's specs, and was going to jump on them when she decided it would be better to put them on her Mum's nose instead, so that somebody, anybody, please, might see the ghost beside herself. She looked round for Fishy, but he was busy, singing songs of love to Bomber. Chris was out playing football, of course. She wandered into his room, which he'd forgotten to lock against her, and jumped on his latest model of a battleship, but didn't get much joy out of it. Strange, just lately she didn't enjoy smashing things so much. Sad, really. She couldn't be growing up, could she? That would be horrific. At last, she picked up Baby Fred and sang funny songs to him which he laughed at hugely, showing his new teeth, and patting her face with pudgy hands.

"I found your specs," she told her mother, who came hurrying in. "You'd better put them on and then you can see the ghost properly."

"You're a good girl. You're being very helpful."

She dropped kisses on Mandy's and Fred's heads, which made Mandy furious, through Fred chortled and kicked his fat feet.

"I just wish you'd stop talking about that ghost as if he was real," she called over her shoulder as she trotted off once more. Slitting her eyes, Mandy tucked Fred under one arm and set off to change all the labels round on the Bronze and Iron Age pots.

"That should baffle them," she thought, wandering back to the kitchen, where she remembered her mother hiding some glacé cherries so they wouldn't be eaten before she had time to make a cake for Chris's birthday. She soon found them. Baby Fred enjoyed his cherries, too; it wasn't easy for him, but he champed away with his new teeth, little red trickles running down his chin.

Some ran on to the newspaper and, watching them, Mandy's eye was caught by two words – ULTIMATE DETERRENT – now what did that mean? Something to do with last, she thought, an end something – that's what I need for the ghost, an ultimate deterrent, a final, finishing him off for good, cheerio, Ghost. Yes, she must think up something, something spectacular, something great, the ultimate ghost deterrent.

But she didn't know what, as yet.

After the weekend, school was awful. School's ghastly and home's ghostly, she thought bitterly as she sat barricaded with chairs in a corner of the classroom, so that Cressy Gale's gang couldn't get at her, she hoped. With Hallowe'en near, the children had been writing stories and poems full of witches, wizards and warlocks, and making their party spook outfits.

"We don't need to make a witch with a broomstick this year," sniggered Carol Moore, "when we got 'er, ole Witchie-Batty-Four-Eyes." This name was taken up with glee by that part of the class with nothing better to do. Cries of "Where's your broomstick, then? Give's a ride," were heard.

A dead mouse appeared in her shoe bag, a live frog in her desk. Mandy remembered how funny she'd once thought it when she'd put one in Chris's bed, but that was a trick she wouldn't play any more, for now she felt sorry for the frog. Unfair to frogs. She carried it, throbbing and always at the point of jumping, back to the pond near the tower.

"Witches always have toads or frogs or things like

that," Cressy Cale called after her. But Mandy ignored her. Holding the frog carefully, she thought about the ultimate deterrent. What were the ultimately bad things? Plagues, she supposed, the dreaded Black Death, rabies, nuclear bombs, germ warfare, poison gas. All very nasty. But not the kind of thing that Mandy Phillips could use against a ghost or a gang. Vampires and werewolves, ogres and monsters, all jolly good in their way, but not what she needed now.

The frog was settled safely by the pond, and Mandy continued homewards, thinking, thinking. When Mandy got her teeth into something she didn't let go easily.

In the kitchen rose a delectable smell. Her father and mother and Fred were enjoying toasted buns. With lashings of jam.

"School trips," said her father. "That's what we need. Plenty of school trips."

"School trips are dreadful. I'm sorry for the teachers. When I helped last year I was completely shattered. I just wanted to disappear from the face of the earth . . . Hello, Mandy. How was your day?"

Mandy wasn't answering that question.

"Dad. Dad. Dad. Dad," she was shouting.

"Yes. Yes. Yes. Yes," he replied.

"School trip. Can we have one? Soon? From school to here? Can we be the first school trip? Please, oh, please?"

"Yes. I don't see why not. I'll write to your teacher. What made you think of it?"

Mandy's face split into a grin that stretched from ear to ear.

"It'll be my ultimate deterrent," she said. And she kissed Fred on his well-buttered cheek.

14

On a warm and golden October afternoon the Blue Addlesbury Tourer wound its way round the steep and
winding Addlesbury lanes, carrying the two top classes
of Addlesbury Primary up to visit the clock tower and its
museum.

"An excellent idea," Miss Fairhead had said in reply to
Mr. Phillips's invitation. And Wednesday afternoon
was decided upon, free of charge for this special opening
invitation to the local school. This nicely scotched Cressy
Gale's comment:

"I'm not paying to see Batty's stupid old ghost."

"I'm scared," said someone else.

"I hope we see it," said the girl who loved nightmares.

A letter to the parents indicated that the trip was for
educational purposes, part of the History and Environ-
mental Studies for that term. Parents were also invited,
but they had to pay the entrance fee.

"I shan't go," announced Cressy to her gang. "Who
wants to go near that rotten dump?"

But she was there all the same, as the children lined up
with clipboards and pencils, packed teas, and a small
amount of money each for souvenirs.

Miss Fairhead sat by Amanda. No one else would. The
team, Chris included, sat in the back seats, singing songs
and cheering as they left the village. Miss Fairhead was
an old hand at school trips, and had supplied buckets for
those throwing up and plasters for those falling down.
Nothing was to be eaten before exploring the tower, all

to be kept for tea afterwards. Mr. Browning and six parents were helping. Nothing could go wrong. She hoped. Quite soon the coach stopped outside the clock tower.

Mr. Phillips now came to show them round. The ground floor, with its prehistory treasures, its stuffed animals and cases of coins was now looking quite different from when he had first arrived there. Everything was clearly labelled, there were posters on the wall, and a small souvenir stall (beside which Baby Fred gurgled in his pram, lovely, lovely, bubbly, guggly, children, lots of, ran his happy Fred thoughts).

Mr. Phillips intended taking them round the various floors first, then six at a time round the parapet, before going down to tea. As she sold souvenirs to the children her mother noticed that Amanda was giving an excellent imitation of a saint.

"Isn't she being good?" she thought. "But perhaps she's always good at school. Perhaps it's only with us that she's so tiresome." She sighed at this, then decided to cheer up, for it was a lovely afternoon and they seemed nice children. She didn't notice Carol Moore picking up two souvenirs and paying for only one. Nor Cressy Gale pinching Mandy and Mandy quietly twisting her left little finger in return.

Souvenirs purchased, the exhibits on the ground floor were examined and explained by Mr. Phillips, after which they trooped up to the first floor with its pictures and paintings, old musical instruments and even older books, some of them chained to the shelves. It was all so peaceful, the children busy making notes and drawings, clipboards in position, Mr. Phillips talking happily to them.

"Jolly good," thought Mr. Browning.

"A successful outing," thought Miss Fairhead.

"I do like school trips," thought Mr. Phillips, pausing for them all to look at a harpsichord covered with paintings of extravagantly dressed men and women wandering in flowery gardens.

Then up past the flat went the visitors, except for Mandy, who slid in and out of her kitchen quick as a flash, and was back with the crowd in time to hear Cressy say:

"That baby's too nice to be *her* brother. And her Dad's all right. Adopted, that's what she is."

For a moment, Mandy felt stricken. But she rallied, Amanda fashion. No time to worry about that now. She'd think about it later.

And now they approached the armoury.

"This is a particularly interesting room," her father was saying. "In here we have the armour and weapons collected by King Cole himself. And while the boys are investigating these, the girls will enjoy looking at the hand-embroidered tapestries hanging on the walls . . ."

"Oh, really," thought Mandy, "not these girls . . ." as she walked softly towards a certain clumsy suit of armour inside which a certain invisible ghost was grumbling peevishly to himself at the disturbance. Crook, also invisible, watched from the perch on the helmet.

It was a perfect English afternoon, with the autumn sunlight streaming through the stained-glass windows. Mr. Phillips pointed out a specially fine cross-bow. The Mums wondered how anyone had the patience to do so much embroidery. Miss Fairhead reminded herself that she must remember to tip the coach driver. Mr. Browning felt pleased that he was not wearing a suit of armour on a hot day.

Mandy Phillips was now just beside the suit of armour. Cressy Gale, watching her closely, crept right behind her to see what she was up to. Behind her was Carol Moore, and the girl who loved nightmares.

Mandy Phillips lifted up the visor, and taking the pepperpot she'd fetched from her kitchen she emptied all its contents right into the suit of armour, and retreated to a far corner as fast as she could. This was rather faster than Crook, who tried to flap to the window but too late.

Like a volcano erupting in the ocean and creating a new island, King Cole erupted from the armour, materialized, waved desperate arms in the air, and sneezed and sneezed and sneezed and went on sneezing, mainly over Cressy. Some sneezes blessed Carol and a few rained upon the nightmare girl but most fell on Cressy. Crook's feathers flew, a rotting stench rose in the air, and the gentle autumn chilled rapidly to a Siberian winter. All the afternoon peace was shattered as King Cole was revealed to Addlesbury Primary in all his glory, and he, in turn, saw many Mandys; a horrible ghost, terrible demons. Wedging a despairing screech between sneezes, he vanished into his armour followed swiftly by Crook, somewhat short of feathers. It was all he needed. Children shrieked and ran for the door. The grown-ups, directed by Miss Fairhead, keeping very cool, managed to guide them safely down the stairs and on to the coach, where order was restored and they had their tea. Mandy stayed still in the far corner of the armoury.

The ultimate deterrent had succeeded beyond her wildest dreams. King Cole and the Addlesbury Gang had scared the wits out of each other.

But her Dad, his golden afternoon ruined, stood lost and bewildered in the middle of the room, his carefully prepared notes strewn on the floor. All around lay clipboards, pencils and abandoned souvenirs. And as he and Mandy looked at one another, her Mum came in,

holding Fred, his starfish hands waving at Mandy and the sunlight.

Her Dad? *Her* Mum? *Her* Baby Fred? No.

She understood now. And didn't like what she understood. She knew why she was different from her gentle family. Knew why she looked like that ghost. She didn't know the details, but she knew now that she was descended from HIM. She was adopted. Everything made sense. She was like him, and that was why no one liked her, had ever liked her.

"Well," said Mr. Phillips at last, with just the trace of a grin. "Even if the clock tower museum enterprise is wrecked, you were certainly right, Mandy. You proved there is a ghost."

Mandy sank down on the floor, covered her face with her hands, and cried and cried.

15

Mandy had been put to bed early with a warm drink and an aspirin, and had fallen asleep without telling her father and mother what was really bothering her. They were upset at finding that the tower actually was haunted, and sat up for a long time talking about what they ought to do, Mrs. Phillips wanting to leave next day, Mr. Phillips saying let's wait, it'll be all right, for he was ready to do anything except leave his beloved tower. The events of the afternoon would probably prevent the museum being a success, but he wanted to carry on as if nothing had happned, and perhaps the ghost would go away and the visitors come eventually.

"I don't know what to do for the best," sighed his

wife. "But I do know I'm not going to bed without you. He might visit me in the night."

But it wasn't her he visited.

Shortly after midnight Mandy awoke in a panic. A nightmare, she had had a ghastly nightmare. Baby Fred was in great danger! Her Fred! (She had forgotten that she'd cried herself to sleep because he wasn't hers any more.) If he was in danger she must save him. So unused was she to this scared, panicky sensation that made her inside slither up and down that she nearly forgot her specs. Remembering them in time, she padded in bare and rapidly cooling feet along to Fred's little room, from which a sickly green glow shone underneath the door.

I know you're there, she thought, angrily. How dare you frighten Fred? Why, if you've hurt him, I'll, I'll exterminate you . . . and then remembered she couldn't.

She flung open the door instead.

And there in the green glow stood Fred, hanging on to the bars of his cot, four new chompers well on view as he beamed cheerily and stamping his fat feet, rings of damp curls lying flat over his head, nice googly-goo, gurgly-wurgly, wiggly, ghosty-woasty, pretty, pretty buggley-boo, and now, here, look, it's Mandy too, grin, grin, stamp, stamp, six raspberries all in a row, prrht, purrht.

"Oh, Fred," she cried and grabbed him.

With Fred clasped to her shoulder, Mandy and the ghost stared hard at each other for what seemed like eternity. At last, the ghost gave a despairing wail and, turning away, hurled himself through Fred's window, down, down, down, splat, ouch.

She laid Fred down, kissed him and covered him up warmly. Then she ran downstairs. The night was bitterly cold. So were her feet. But she didn't notice. She was far more interested in the sobbing, mouldy form lying at her feet, Crook beside him.

"What is it?" she asked, bending down.

"I'm so old and tired," groaned the ghost. "So tired. How would you like to be a hundred and fifty years old and aching all over? Even my thoughts ache. And I'm such a failure. Just think – " he laughed wildly into the night, startling two nearby rabbits – "I can't even frighten a baby. A baby. I knew I couldn't frighten you, girl or demon or whatever you are, but fancy not being able to frighten a baby! For a ghost, that's the end, except it isn't unfortunately. It goes on and on and on and on..."

His voice trailed miserably away.

"You frightened my class all right," Mandy said, trying to be encouraging.

"Not half as much as they frightened me."

"What about all those people you were supposed to have frightened to death?"

"All lies. I wasn't anywhere near them at the time. People said it just to have me sound worse than I am. I've never killed anyone. I know I was a nasty old man, but I'm not some sort of murderer."

"Why were you so horrible to me then?"

"I wanted you all to go away."

"I see."

"But it doesn't seem to matter any more."

He dragged himself up painfully and peered at her. "I'm getting used to you. It was jolly boring and lonely with only Crook for company."

"You can say that again," Crook joined in with feeling.

"I feel that way as well, so I suppose you may as well stay here and haunt us. You didn't bother me much, anyway," said Mandy.

"Yes, but you see, I'm awfully tired," said King Cole. "It's been a long time."

"What do you want to do, then?"

"I want to rest properly, in my vault in Addlesbury churchyard," He brightened up for a moment. "It's awfully handsome. I had it made specially, and it's got urns and my coat of arms on it. You should go and have a look at it some time."

"Well, why don't you go there, then?"

"There's something I've got to do before I can rest. And it's all so long ago I find it difficult to remember. Oh, I know. I've got to find out who pushed me off the tower. For the Records Office, you know. But I can't find out. I never knew how to set about it at all. Who could? It's so long ago."

"But I know who could," cried Amanda. "My Dad can find out anything. He's brilliant at it." (She'd forgotten all about thinking he wasn't really her Dad.) "Mr. Cole," she spoke respectfully to him, at last. "You can go and rest now. I'll do everything I can to help you."

"Come on, Coley. I want to go to sleep," yawned Crook.

16

Mandy woke up determined to ask her parents when she was adopted and why hadn't they told her? Then she would direct her father into finding out all about Mr. Cole and why he fell off the tower, and did he fall or was he pushed? She would get things moving.

Her mother awoke after shocking nightmares, determined to tell her husband that she and the children couldn't possibly be expected to spend their lives in a haunted tower, and could they leave it as soon as possible, please?

The phone rang while Mr. Phillips was making toast, for he was up first. A voice said:

"*Addlesbury and District News* here. Is it all right if I

come and have a chat to you some time today? And is it all right for me to take pictures of the tower? And the ghost, ha ha?''

"Well, yes," said Mr. Phillips, surprised, rescuing his toast which the toaster had just hurled contemptuously on to the floor. He put down the receiver and the 'phone rang again.

"Mr. Phillips? Oh-oh, jo-lly good. I'm from the *Haunted Times* and I wondered could I come and have a look, you know, at the jo-lly old ghost? The one in your tower? All right? Jo-lly good. And would it be all right if I brought some jo-lly old equipment along, tapes, you know, and what-not?"

"I suppose so," said Mr. Phillips, even more surprised, looking sadly at his blackened toast.

His wife came in, tired and pale. Fishy also slipped furtively in.

"Bill," began Mrs. Phillips.

"Why is Fishy making that awful noise?" cried Mandy, coming in. A mouse ran across the floor, revealing itself and the reason for Fishy's awful noise.

"For goodness sake," cried Mr. Phillips.

"Mandy, get both the cat and the mouse out of here!" cried her mother.

Mandy dived into action as Chris rushed in, obviously in a hurry.

"I'm late. Where's my kit? Where's my breakfast?"

"Bill, you surely don't expect me to live here with a ghost?" cried Mrs. Phillips, not her usual self at all.

"Come, come, puss puss, naughty Fishy," called Mandy.

"You've finished all the Ricicles, you beast. You know they're my favourite."

"No, I didn't, so there. Come on, Fishy, there, got you, out you go."

The phone rang. Three coachloads of visitors would be arriving. Could lunch be provided?

"Bill, are you listening? I want to leave here."

"Marilyn," cried her husband. "There isn't time to leave at the moment. About a hundred and fifty visitors are arriving. And two lots of reporters."

Mrs. Phillips burst into tears.

"I've got the mouse," shouted Mandy. "What shall I do with it?"

"Oh, just get rid of it somewhere," said her father, who thought he was going demented.

"Mum, stop crying. I want my breakfast. And my kit. Please."

"Now, everybody, listen to ME," shouted Mandy, who'd decided enough time had been wasted, and she wasn't messing about any longer. "Dad. Mum. Why didn't you tell me I was adopted?"

Complete silence fell, as they all gazed at her, open-mouthed.

Mr. Phillips bowed his head in his hands. And once more, the phone started to ring. Suddenly he yelled, in a voice even louder than Mandy's:

"Of course you're not adopted. It's me that was adopted!"

Mandy's mouth fell open and stayed like that, as her father picked up the receiver, and a cheery cry from above showed that Baby Fred wished to come down to join the fun.

Mandy went to school deep in thought. So did Chris. He was thinking about the afternoon match with Nether Codlington Junior School. She thought about the ghost and her Dad being adopted. It was halfway through the morning before she remembered Cressy Gale and her gang.

"There'll be no trouble from them today," she sniffed to herself.

She was right. They were as quiet as little mice wearing felt slippers. At lunch time Mandy went along to join a newly formed Drama Club, which was hoping to produce a play for the Christmas concert.

"Do you think I could help?" she asked humbly, for she was learning sense at last.

"Perhaps we might let you," they said.

"Have you thought of a play yet?"

"No, not yet," answered Cherry, Chris's girl-friend.

"I know one about a dragon," said Mandy.

"We want a Christmas play," they answered.

"I could . . . I mean we could easily bring Christmas into it."

The members of the Drama Club looked at one another.

"Tell us about it, then," one of them said at last.

Mandy not only told them about it, she roared the famous dragon roar. They were very impressed, for they'd never heard a roar like it. Then they fetched papers and pencils and began to write the play. It was called *The Christmas Dragon* and Mandy's part was the biggest.

At the end of a long and busy day, Mandy sat talking to the ghost very quietly in her bedroom. He was keeping out of the way of people from the Society of Psychical Research (ghost-spotters) who were fixing tape recorders, bits of thread and so on all over the tower. Her father had had a busy day, too, but he had found time to have a talk with Mandy.

"So you see, I look like you 'cos you're my great-great-great – I'm not sure how many greats, I haven't worked it out yet, grandfather. Dad says I'm a throwback. He was lucky not looking like you.''

"I'm not so ill-looking as all that," snapped the ghost.

"Yes, you look better than you did at first. I must have got used to you. When Dad told me I thought that meant WE owned the tower, but he said your son sold it, and he spent all his money anyway, and there was none left."

"How absolutely disgusting! Spending MY money, indeed. How dare he!"

"It wouldn't be much use to you, now."

"I suppose not. But I don't like to think I don't own the tower any more!"

"Do you want to hear the rest? How Dad's real parents came over here for a holiday and were killed in a train smash, and he was adopted by Mr. and Mrs. Phillips, and took their name and they're Gran and Grandad, to me that is, and they live up North now, but they're coming to stay when it's all sorted out 'cos my Grandad wants to see the clock tower again, where he used to wind up the clock, though that was nothing to do with my dad being descended from you. Are you listening?"

"No, it's very boring."

"Well, there's just one thing I want to know. Why didn't you haunt them?"

"I don't haunt on Sunday mornings which is when he wound it up. I saw him once or twice but I kept out of his way mostly. It was because you decided to live here that I wanted to get rid of you."

"I think it's interesting. Coincidence, my Dad said. That's a good word. Where have you gone?"

The ghost had disappeared. Only Crook sat fast asleep on the dressing table.

"I was bored," said King Cole, reappearing. "And I've had a horrible day, people everywhere, and now you tell me I don't own the tower. I'm sick of it all. You go on and on, talking about those wretched descendants of mine who spent all my money and I don't give a fig for them. What I want to know is who pushed me off the parapet."

"Lots of people must have wanted to," snorted Mandy. "You're so rude."

"What about you?"

"I'm trying to improve. I let Chris have first pick of the cakes at tea time."

But the ghost wasn't listening.

"I want to know what your father's going to find out about me."

"He hasn't got much time at the moment with all these people coming here."

"Then you'll have to."

"But I can't."

"Yes, you can. Just as well as your father. Research, it's called."

"I don't know where to begin," cried Mandy.

But she did. She began with the museum and school. She read reports and records and looked at photographs. Then she went to the local newspaper office and read the old papers with their accounts of the tower being built, the opening celebrations and the mysterious death of the eccentric folly builder.

"You were mean and horrible just as I thought," she told the ghost, later. "There's a story in one paper that you didn't pay the builders the money you promised them. And you got one of your servants sent to prison for something he hadn't done anyway, as they found out afterwards. I bet nobody could stand you, not your wife nor your son, nor your neighbours, nor the servants, and certainly not the workmen. Any one of them might have pushed you off. But it doesn't seem as if they did, for they were all somewhere else at the time and you were alone."

"Huh," snorted the ghost. "That's not much use. And I don't see why I should be hated like that. Lots of people were just as bad."

"You're not lots of people. You're you. Aren't you sorry?"

He shuffled sulkily. "Since I'm being punished for it, yes," and then he and Crook vanished, for they could hear the approach of ghost-spotters again.

❦ The End ❦

Mandy returned to the newspaper office yet once more in the hope of finding something she'd missed. But at last she sat back and sighed, for she still had no clue as to who had actually pushed the hated millionaire off the tower on that day long ago. She handed back the old and yellowing paper, absent-mindedly reading the headline on the back page as she did so. 'Freak wind hits Addlesbury only,' it said.

Back at the tower, her father was hanging up a picture on the ground floor.

"Do you like it?" he asked, standing back.

"What is it?"

"It's an old print of Addlesbury Hill before our ghostly ancestor decided to build on it. That's the stone circle that stood here, apparently, though there's no sign of it today, and the rampart surrounding it seems to have been flattened, and the trees cut down. I've heard it said that what made him so hated by the villagers, among other things, was destroying that circle. They said it was magic, the old villagers did, and that he'd taken away their good luck."

Mandy went upstairs in search of food, her brain beavering away frantically, as she chomped her way through three helpings of chicken casserole followed by treacle tart without really noticing what she was eating. Then, after inspecting Baby Fred's latest tooth and helping with the washing up, she lay on her bed and thought and thought. And fell asleep.

A cloud passed in front of the moon, sending dark shadows over the tower and Addlesbury Hill. A shiver of fear ran through the wood, a sense of deep unease. Birds flew to their nests, animals ran to their holes. Bomber gathered her five beautiful new kittens towards her and wrapped herself round them protectively, while Fishy, pausing in his hunting, started to run to them.

Mandy was dreaming. In her dreams she saw mile after mile of wooded hills, and then one particular hill, familiar in shape, a circle of stones set in its top like a necklace, encircled in turn by a deep rampart.

And suddenly the trees were flattened by a rushing, whirling wind, the stones fell down, and the circle was destroyed.

"That's it," she cried in her sleep and woke to find King Cole and Crook beside her.

"You were blown off," she said, sitting up. "Can you remember?"

Rage and pain chased across the ghost's face. He could remember, now.

"I stood on the parapet gloating. I'd just bought up some more land. And this terrible . . ." he shivered as he thought of it . . . "awful wind swirled up from inside the tower and I found myself flying through the air. They didn't find me for two days. They just thought I'd gone off in one of my rages." He sank wearily on to the floor, then continued:

"And that's why they didn't know it was the wind. They seemed to think I'd jumped off. As if I'd do such a thing."

"But what about the stones?" asked Mandy.

"What stones?"

"The stone circle."

"Oh, that. I had them smashed up and built them into the tower. After all, they were here already, whereas all the rest had to be hauled up the hill. I was proud of that. It saved a bit of money."

Mandy stared at him in horror and astonishment.

"But — but the villagers thought they were magic. They were old and sacred."

"I don't believe in that silly rubbish."

"Well, you better begin, for I think they really pushed you off, and somehow we must get them to let you go." Mandy's fighting look spread over her face and she pushed up her glasses which had gone a bit crooked because she'd fallen asleep in them. "Come on," she cried, "let's go on the parapet. And look out for ghost-spotters."

She crept as furtively as she could up to the parapet, her invisible companions close behind. No ghost-spotters were to be seen.

Up there above the trees, the stars bright in the sky, the hills just visible and everything still, the world looked very beautiful and Mandy wondered why the ghost wanted to leave it. But as he materialized beside her she realized how old and tired he was. Then she had the most peculiar feeling that all that world she could see, the Addlesbury world, was waiting for something, for something to happen, for HER, in fact. I'm on a stage, she thought, a great, big stage.

She stepped forward as far as she could, and lifted her arms.

"Let him go," she cried in her loudest, most enormous, Amanda Phillips the Mighty voice, and then, softly, "for he's sorry, truly he is."

Somewhere in the tower a faint stirring began. Mandy turned and nudged King Cole.

"Say you're sorry," she hissed. "Quick. And don't forget to take him with you. I don't want to be left with him." She pushed Crook under the ghost's arm. Trembling violently, he opened his mouth. Not a sound emerged.

"Don't be afraid," cried Mandy.

At that moment the parapet door flew open, and an eager group of ghost-spotters burst into view.

"Quick, quick," she cried once more.

"I'm sorry. Please forgive me!" he cried.

There came a wild scream from the depths of the tower, which shook and shuddered as a wind of enormous violence tore through it and out to the woods and hills beyond. Mandy clung to the parapet wall, her eyes shut, praying, as the ghost, mouldy shroud billowing like a great sail, flew over the wall and fell down, down, down, on his last leap.

Screams and cries of "It's the ghost," were coming from the spotters, all clutching one another, but Mandy was peering down to where her ghost lay. To her it seemed that he was looking at her and he even seemed to be saying something, which she thought was "Goodbye, and love, great-great-great-great-great..." and then there was nothing on the ground at all, nothing at all.

On a bright and sunny day some months later, the Phillipses (Baby Fred standing on his own two feet), Addlesbury Primary School and a crowd of visitors waited outside the clock tower. At noon the new carillon rang out loud and clear over the trees and the hills to the astonished birds.

"Good old King Cole,
God rest his soul."

Mandy nodded approvingly to her many admirers at the school before grinning at her Dad.

"I think he'll like that," she said, before leading the way inside to the lunch that had been put out ready for them.

The End (well, possibly)